The Counting Sheepdog

Written and
Illustrated by
Eric M. Strong

One day in Scotland, in the Isle of Skye
a sheep dog lie napping, his flock nearby.

He rolled to his back, from his back to his side
he woke up bushy tailed, but not bright eyed.

5

Then up snapped his head,
soon quickly he stood
For a shepherd to doze was simply no good!

7

8

"Oh me ! Oh my! I've done it again!"
To make sure no lamb was missing
he counted all ten.

9

"Three is Nessie, four counting Cid"
wiping and rubbing his heavy eye lids.

"Five is Roosevelt, six will be Sean"
counting these sheep was making him yawn.

15

"Seven is Ginger, eight is Lenore"
barely awake he started to snore.

"Nine is Duncan, ten is Nancine"
counting his last, he started to dream.

And fast asleep he fell like a log,
for it's hard to stay up
when you're a counting sheepdog.

About the Illustrator
Eric lives to create narratives that help underdogs exceed their wildest dreams!

With over 20 years of professional experience as a freelance artist he has worked on over 60 children's books, 400 hundred animations, and thousands of professional illustrations. He has worked for many large companies but his favorite clients are self-publishing authors and small studios.

For more informartion visit:
ericmstrong.com

Made in United States
Troutdale, OR
11/14/2024

24843751R00017